AF382212

ÉMILE ZOLA

The father of naturalism

Written by Julie Pihard
In collaboration with Anne-Sophie Close
Translated by Rebecca Neal

Art & Literature 50MINUTES.com

ÉMILE ZOLA

- **Name:** Émile Édouard Charles Antoine Zola.
- **Born:** 2 April 1840 in Paris.
- **Died:** 29 September 1902 in Paris.
- **Context:** during the second half of the 19th century, Europe was gradually entering the modern era as a direct consequence of the Industrial Revolution and the rise of capitalism. At this time, a heightened form of realism emerged in art and literature, with the aim of representing everyday life as faithfully as possible.
- **Notable works:**
  - *Thérèse Raquin* (1867), novel
  - *The Belly of Paris* (1873), novel
  - *L'Assommoir* (1877), novel
  - *Nana* (1880), novel
  - *The Ladies' Paradise* (1883), novel
  - *Germinal* (1885), novel
  - *The Human Beast* (1890), novel
  - *Doctor Pascal* (1893), novel

Over 100 years after his death, Émile Zola's name

still holds an important place in the collective imagination. He was one of the most popular French writers of his time and remains one of the most widely read, translated and studied authors in the world. He was the leading figure of naturalism, a literary movement which sought to apply the scientific method to writing, as he laid the movement's theoretical foundations and popularised it. During his lifetime, his work was met with unprecedented enthusiasm: it had a major impact on and garnered effusive praise from the public and critics alike, and his writing style remained the dominant model for the next several decades.

In addition to his talent as a writer, Zola had a keen eye for the truth. This can be seen in his books, and especially in his sprawling 20-novel familial and social history *Les Rougon-Macquart* (1871-1893), which provides a meticulous depiction of the world, society and its various social classes. His search for the truth is also made evident by his political and social commitment, and in particular in his role in the Dreyfus affair. Zola threw his support behind Alfred Dreyfus, an army officer who was wrongfully accused of leaking French military secrets and wrote his famous pamphlet *J'accuse...!* ("I accuse...!", 1898) in his defence. As both a literary genius and a staunch opponent of injustice in all its forms, Zola's reputation reached almost mythical proportions, and he remains a beloved figure today.

CONTEXT

FROM MONARCHY TO EMPIRE TO REPUBLIC

The 19th century in general was a period of major upheaval, and this was also true during Zola's lifetime. Having spent his childhood in the countryside, far from the concerns of the July Monarchy (1830-1848), he arrived in Paris in 1848, the year that the Second Republic, led by Louis-Napoléon Bonaparte (1808-1873), the nephew of Napoleon Bonaparte (1769-1821), was established. However, this regime was short-lived: Bonaparte launched a coup d'état in December 1851 and founded the Second French Empire (a regime that Zola hated) in 1852. He proclaimed himself emperor, adopted the name Napoleon III, established an authoritarian regime, profoundly modernised the country and sought to expand French territory.

However, France's defeat in the Franco-Prussian War (1870-1871) dealt the death blow to the

Empire's prestige, and in in 1870 it was replaced by the Third Republic. This was the first sustained period of relative stability since the French Revolution in 1789 and lasted until 1940. However, the new regime was not met with universal acceptance in its early days: there was an uprising in Paris from March to May 1871, partly because the city's inhabitants did not want to submit to the victorious Prussians. This revolt, known as the Paris Commune, was violently repressed by Adolphe Thiers' (1797-1877) government in a series of brutal attacks. The insurrection came to an end after *La semaine sanglante* ("The Bloody Week") from 21 to 28 May 1871 and resulted in the loss of an estimated 20 000 lives. After this upheaval, the National Assembly was reluctant to implement any abrupt changes, and took nine years to finalise the new regime's laws and constitution. These new legal precepts were strongly influenced by modernisation and incorporated previously controversial subjects such as the rights to secularism, strike action and freedom of assembly.

EVOLUTIONS AND REVOLUTIONS ON THE ROAD TO MODERNITY

In addition to the political instability that characterised the 19th century, Europe also experienced a period of rapid economic development as a result of the Industrial Revolution, which began in Britain at the start of the century. In France, it reached its peak during the July Monarchy and especially under the Second Empire. The country underwent its most radical changes during the reign of Napoleon III: with the help of the prefect Baron Haussmann (1809-1891), the Emperor radically altered the layout of Paris with a view to improving hygiene, protecting citizens and boosting the city's prestige; the first department stores opened; transport developed considerably; mass production and the production line emerged; and major industries appeared. All these factors contributed to the rise of capitalism, which was still in its infancy at this time.

Industrialisation also led to the emergence of a new social class, the urban proletariat, which was examined in detail by Zola and was responsible for significant social advances throughout the 19th century. The most important of these advances took place during the Third Republic, which promulgated the first legislation concerning workers' rights: trade unions were legalised and labour political parties were created to support them. As a result, working conditions gradually became less difficult (for example, a mandatory daily break was introduced in 1906), child labour was now regulated, and workers gained the right to strike and the opportunity to retire and end their lives in greater comfort and security. Furthermore, primary education was now free, and was made compulsory in 1882 through laws introduced by Jules Ferry (1832-1893).

THE EMERGENCE OF SOCIALISM

In the 1830s, socialism, the best-known version of which was developed by Karl Marx (1818-1883), emerged in France as a direct consequence of the workers' movement and the need for new social provisions. Its aim was to combat injustice, poverty and the class system, and to fight for equality for all and the fair distribution of property.

THE VENERATION OF SCIENCE AND HISTORY

The 19th century also saw great leaps forward and major discoveries in the field of science, which had an effect on all areas of knowledge, including literature. Charles Darwin (1809-1882) developed his highly controversial theory of evolution, while Prosper Lucas (1808-1885), who had a considerable influence on Zola, put forward his theories on heredity and degeneration. At the same time, important work was being carried out by Louis Pasteur (1822-1895), the pioneer of microbiology and the inventor of the rabies vaccine, and Pierre (1859-1906) and Marie (1867-1934) Curie, the Nobel Prize-winning physicists who garnered recognition for their research on radium. In medicine, the experimental method was theorised and tested by the physiologist Claude Bernard (1813-1878) in the second half of the century. Zola was directly inspired by Bernard's work when he wrote his *Les Rougon-Macquart* cycle.

| Portrait of Claude Bernard.

In a broader sense, science came to be held in much higher esteem in the 19th century. Furthermore, positivism, a school of thought developed in the first half of the century by the

French philosopher Auguste Comte (1798-1857) which theorised that phenomena could only be explained by observation and experience, became more popular. This led to introspective and intuitive approaches being completely discredited. At the end of the century, scientism, an offshoot of positivism, asserted that science can reveal the truth about everything in existence and provide solutions to all human problems.

Finally, the 19th century was also the century of history: people became aware that history is written in the present and that the past is vital, as it facilitates the understanding of contemporary events and bolsters a country's prestige. Nationalism also developed in this period as each country sought to assert itself and extol the characteristics that made it unique. This enthusiasm for history is particularly evident in literature and other art forms. Alexandre Dumas (1802-1870) wrote historical novels set in bygone eras; with Zola a generation later there was a shift in perspective, as authors rewrote contemporary history as a way of assimilating and making sense of it.

19TH-CENTURY LITERATURE: FROM IDEALISM TO REALISM

In the 19th century, culture finally became more accessible to the general public. Previously, creators had relied on patrons who were generally politicians and used art for their own ends, but in this period culture became independent of the state thanks to writers such as Victor Hugo (1802-1885), who had no qualms about criticising the powers that be. Artists were now considered to be free and took on a new status: they became professionals and economic agents in their own right. For ordinary citizens, access to education went hand in hand with access to culture, which was now disseminated widely thanks to popular newspapers which provided cultural information and published serialised novels.

The dawn of the 19th century was dominated by two major literary movements: Romanticism, which was at its height between 1820 and 1848, and realism, which became more popular between 1850 and 1870. The most prominent Romantic writers in France included Alphonse de Lamartine (1790-1869), Victor Hugo and Alfred de Musset (1810-1857), and the movement was characterised by heightened sensibility, the foregrounding of emotion and passion, and the rejection of modern society in favour of a return to humankind's roots through contemplation, the exaltation of the past and love for nature. Realism counted Stendhal (1783-1842), Honoré de Balzac (1799-1850) and Gustave Flaubert (1821-1880) among its main proponents and differed from Romanticism because of its severity, authentic tone and focus on truth and objectivity. Realist works aimed to denounce injustice, were often based on considerable documentary research, and provided meticulously detailed descriptions of people and their environments.

Zola breathed new life into realism and made the movement more radical with the development of naturalism. He drew inspiration from Prosper Lucas's theories on heredity and aimed to apply Claude Bernard's experimental method to novel-writing. In this way, his self-described "experimental novel" was a sort of laboratory which mixed biology and history to determine the characters' behaviour and future. His famous *Les Rougon-Macquart* series, which he subtitled

The Natural and Social History of a Family Under the Second Empire, was a pioneering naturalist project. While Zola was undeniably the originator, leading theorist and most important representative of the movement, several other authors adopted a similar approach for a time, including the Goncourt brothers (Edmond, 1822-1896 and Jules, 1830-1870), Alphonse Daudet (1840-1897) and Guy de Maupassant (1850-1893).

In the late 19th century, naturalism began to fade away, but it did not disappear completely and endured until the early 20th century. Between 1880 and 1900, it was superseded by Symbolism, which turned away from reality to return to a dreamy lyricism with marked mystical influences. The best-known writers in this idealistic new movement were Stéphane Mallarmé (1842-1898), Paul Verlaine (1844-1896) and Arthur Rimbaud (1854-1891).

BIOGRAPHY

| Portrait of Émile Zola.

FROM ROMANTIC IDEALISM TO REALIST DISILLUSIONMENT

Émile Zola was born in Paris on 2 April 1840, although he spent most of his childhood in Aix-en-Provence, where his family moved in 1843. His father was an engineer of Venetian descent and died of pneumonia when the future writer was just seven years old, while his mother was a French citizen. He studied at the Collège Bourbon, where he met and became friends with Paul Cézanne (1839-1906), who went on to become a celebrated Impressionist painter.

At the age of 18, after spending his entire youth in rural France, he moved to Paris, where he attended the Lycée Saint-Louis and studied for a baccalaureate in science. However, when he failed his exams he abandoned his studies. The years that followed were not easy for him, as his homesickness in the capital, nostalgia for the countryside, lack of enthusiasm for his studies and poorly-paid work as a clerk for a shipping firm left him demoralised. Previously, he had developed an interest in Romanticism, and in particular in the works of Lamartine and Hugo, but his failures left him more inclined towards the classical, realist impersonality and coolness that characterised the work of authors such as Jules Michelet (1798-1874) and George Sand (1804-1876).

MODEST BEGINNINGS IN THE LITERARY WORLD

The year 1862 marked a turning point in Zola's life, as he secured a job with the publishing company Hachette, first as a clerk, then as head of the advertising department. This work allowed him to mix with many renowned figures from the literary world, including the lexicographer Émile Littré (1801-1881), the literary critic Sainte-Beuve (1804-1869), the philosopher and historian Hippolyte Taine (1828-1893) and the writer Edmond Duranty (1833-1880), and his contact with these figures inspired his dream of becoming a novelist. At this time, he was also reunited with Cézanne, who had moved to Paris and who introduced him to a number of fashionable artists, mainly Impressionists: Camille Pissarro (1830-1903), Alfred Sisley (1839-1899), Claude Monet (1840-1926) and Auguste Renoir (1841-1919).

Zola's first book, *Contes à Ninon*, was rejected by three publishers before being published in 1864. The following year, his first novel, *Claude's Confession*, which also marked his first foray into realism, appeared. This was an intense period of activity for Zola, as he met new people, made new discoveries, read widely and published new material. He also met his future wife, Alexandrine, around this time, and married her in 1870. The couple had no children.

Zola's public declaration of support for scientism at a scientific conference in Aix-en-Provence in 1866 had a considerable impact on his reputation and literary career. The same year, he began writing his major works and decided to make a living from writing alone. He left Hachette and began writing art and literary criticism for various newspapers. His articles were later published in two anthologies in 1865 and 1866. Notably, he was virtually the only contemporary writer to praise Flaubert's *Sentimental Education* (1869), and wrote in defence of the Impressionists.

AMBITIOUS PROJECTS

In 1867, two major events made up for the loss of his position as a critic for the newspaper *L'Événement*: he published a serialised novel, *The Mysteries of Marseilles*, and his first successful work, *Thérèse Raquin*. This marked the beginnings of naturalism, although the movement was not theorised until much later. At this time, he also began to consider writing a collection modelled on Balzac's *The Human Comedy* (1829-1850) which would provide a coherent framework for his different novels. He drew up the plan for this series of novels between 1868 and 1869.

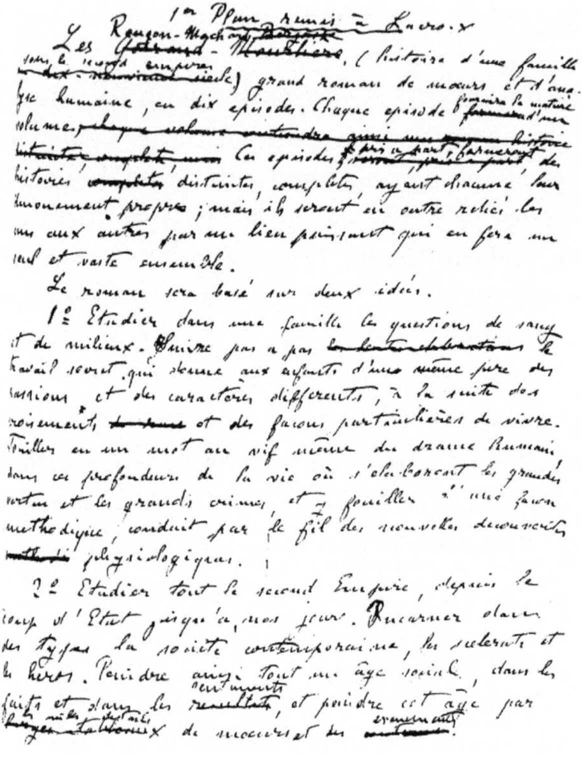

1er Plan remis à Lacroix

Les Rougon-Macquart (histoire d'une famille sous le second empire) grand roman de mœurs et d'analyse humaine, en dix épisodes. Chaque épisode fournira la matière d'un volume. Ces épisodes, pris à part, formeront des histoires distinctes, complètes, ayant chacune leur dénouement propre ; mais ils seront en outre reliés les uns aux autres par un lien puissant qui en fera un seul et vaste ensemble.

Le roman sera basé sur deux idées.

1° Étudier dans une famille les questions de sang et de milieux. Suivre pas à pas le travail secret qui donne aux enfants d'une même père des passions et des caractères différents, à la suite des croisements et des façons particulières de vivre. Fouiller en un mot au vif même du drame humain, dans ces profondeurs de la vie où s'élaborent les grandes vertus et les grands crimes, et y fouiller d'une façon méthodique, conduit par le fil des nouvelles découvertes physiologiques.

2° Étudier tout le second Empire, depuis le coup d'État jusqu'à nos jours. Incarner dans des types la société contemporaine, les scélérats et les héros. Peindre ainsi tout un âge social, dans les faits et dans les sentiments, et peindre cet âge par les mille détails de mœurs et des événements.

| Plan of the *Les Rougon-Macquart* series produced by Zola.

Meanwhile, he discovered Claude Bernard's *Introduction to the Study of Experimental Medicine* (1869), which was a revelation for him and inspired him to apply the scientific principles set out by the doctor to his novels (he wrote an essay about this, *The Experimental Novel*, which was published in 1880). At this time, he also wrote for several opposition newspapers and spoke out against the Second Empire. When Napoleon III was deposed, he moved away from Paris (in particular, he spent time in Bordeaux and Marseilles) for a time and observed the debates of the National Assembly from a distance as a political journalist. After he returned to the capital in 1872, he devoted all his energies to literature and to his monumental *Les Rougon-Macquart* cycle, comprising 20 novels which are connected but can also be read as stand-alone works. This task took him over 20 years.

Zola was a tireless worker and was brimming with ambition. However, he did not reach the peak of his success until 1877 with the publication of *L'Assommoir*. This novel made him the most famous author of his time, both in France and abroad, where his books were translated almost as soon as they were published in French. His next novels – *Nana* (1880), *The Ladies' Paradise* (1883) and above all *Germinal* (1885) – cemented his reputation and his place as the leading figure of naturalism. Furthermore, his 1886 novel *The Masterpiece* led to a falling-out with Cézanne, who felt targeted by the struggling painter depicted in the book. However, Zola was making new friends, namely Flaubert, Edmond and Jules Goncourt, Alphonse Daudet and Guy de Maupassant. In 1878, he bought a house in Médan, which became a key meeting place for the leading naturalist writers. These meetings even gave rise to a naturalist short story collection entitled *Les Soirées de Médan* ("Evenings at Médan") in 1880.

SOCIAL AND POLITICAL COMMITMENT IN HIS LATER YEARS

In 1893, Zola completed the *Les Rougon-Macquart* series with *Doctor Pascal*. He then produced two other cycles: *The Three Cities* (1894-1898), a trilogy in which he tried to dispel his reputation for pessimism by focusing on religious feeling, and *The Four Evangelists* (1899 to his death), an unfinished series combining socialism, religion and justice with metaphorical connections to the Dreyfus affair.

This scandal had a major impact on the final years of Zola's life: the author threw himself into defending Dreyfus with the aim of bringing the truth to light, but his efforts were in vain. As part of this clear-sighted, courageous defence, he wrote his famous open letter *J'accuse...!*, which was published in the French newspaper *L'Aurore* on 13 January 1898. After the letter was published, Zola was sentenced to one year's imprisonment and a 3000-franc fine, which he fled to England to escape. He returned from exile in 1899 for Dreyfus's appeal, after accepting a pardon, and continued to support the officer in the face of fierce opposition.

At the end of 1902, he left his house in Médan for the winter and returned to his apartment in Paris, which had been left uninhabited for months. After lighting and covering the fire, he went to bed with his wife. The following morning, he was found dead, having inhaled toxic fumes caused by a blocked chimney. His wife survived the incident. Even today, some continue to believe that the chimney was blocked deliberately, although there is no way of conclusively proving this.

His death was met with an outpouring of grief

and made headlines around the world. A grand funeral was held on 5 October 1902. The tributes paid to him included those of the writer Anatole France (1844-1924), who described him as "a moment of the conscience of Man", and the group of miners from Denain who followed the funeral procession chanting "Germinal! Germinal!" On 6 June 1908, his ashes were transferred to the Pantheon in a further sign of the esteem in which this great man was held.

The Dreyfus affair

On 15 October 1894, the artillery officer Alfred Dreyfus (1859-1935) was arrested for treason and accused of passing secret French documents to the German Empire. At the time, French society was deeply anti-Semitic, and the fact that Dreyfus was Jewish only fuelled the suspicions against him. On 22 December, he was found guilty and sentenced to life imprisonment on Devil's Island in French Guyana. Although the incident initially received little attention, it made the news around the world when Zola, followed by a number of other authors, spoke out in defence of Dreyfus.

Zola first published an article in *Le Figaro* and a pamphlet in 1897. The following year, *L'Aurore* published *J'accuse...!,* an open letter to Félix Fauré (1841-1899), the President of the Republic at the time, in which Zola denounced the intrigues that marred the trial. After the publication of this letter, the case blew up and split the Third Republic into supporters and opponents of Dreyfus, giving rise to a series of nationalist and anti-Semitic controversies. The second trial also ruled in favour of the military authorities over Dreyfus, but in 1906, after the real guilty parties fled or committed suicide, the truth came out and he was finally exonerated.

| *J'accuse...!*, letter published in the newspaper *L'Aurore* on 13 January 1898.

CHARACTERISTICS OF ZOLA'S WORK

THE BIRTH OF THE EXPERIMENTAL NOVEL

Although the young Zola initially admired Romantic authors, the hardships of life drove him to embrace realism and idolise Balzac, Stendhal and Flaubert. However, before long he came to believe that this aesthetic did not go far enough, and when he came across Claude Bernard and Prosper Lucas's scientific theories, he developed new ideas about describing the world. He was also influenced by the historian Hippolyte Taine, another follower of scientism, who believed that history was an exact science and that it was possible to experiment with it. Finally, when he was working at Hachette, he met a number of positivists, who were characterised by their faith in progress and their belief in empirical knowledge.

These meetings and discoveries planted the seeds of naturalism in Zola. His ambition was to apply Bernard's experimental method, which involved testing a phenomenon through repeated experiments to try and explain it, to literature. Zola therefore tried to understand contemporary history, society and human nature by depicting them in his writing, supporting his work with as much documentation as possible and adopting a particular point of view in each novel. Furthermore, he attempted to demonstrate the hypothesis of double determinism in his works: he believed that humans' characters are shaped by both their environment and circumstances, and their genealogy and the characteristics they inherited from their ancestors. More specifically, in each of his novels he focused on a particular individual and studied the psychological consequences of variables such as their environment, the time period in which they lived and their heredity. This allowed him to create what he called the experimental novel, which he saw as the ideal novel form and which made his reputation.

The descendants of Adélaïde Fouque

In *Les Rougon-Macquart*, all the characters, who span five generations, are connected to Adélaïde Fouque, a woman with a nervous disorder. She had a son with her husband, the sober-minded Rougon, and a son and a daughter with her lover, a smuggler and drunkard named Macquart. The personality traits of Adélaïde and the two men are passed down through the generations and manifest themselves differently depending on the events the character lives through and their environment. In this way, Zola combines fiction and scientific theories on heredity and degeneration in an attempt to prove that there is no dividing line between literature and science.

THE WRITER AS OBSERVER OF REALITY

To write this kind of novel, the writer must above all position themselves as an observer of reality. Naturalism is based on a simple principle: in order to describe a phenomenon, writers must first study it in depth and understand it. For each of his novels, Zola did extensive research on the environments he wanted to describe: he learnt as much as possible about the living conditions and organisational structures there, visited them, conducted interviews, produced documents on the kinds of people he met, drew maps, and so on. This research enabled him to depict a total of over 1200 characters from very varied settings, including the markets of Les Halles, the Church, brothels, department stores and railways, which means that his work has immense documentary value.

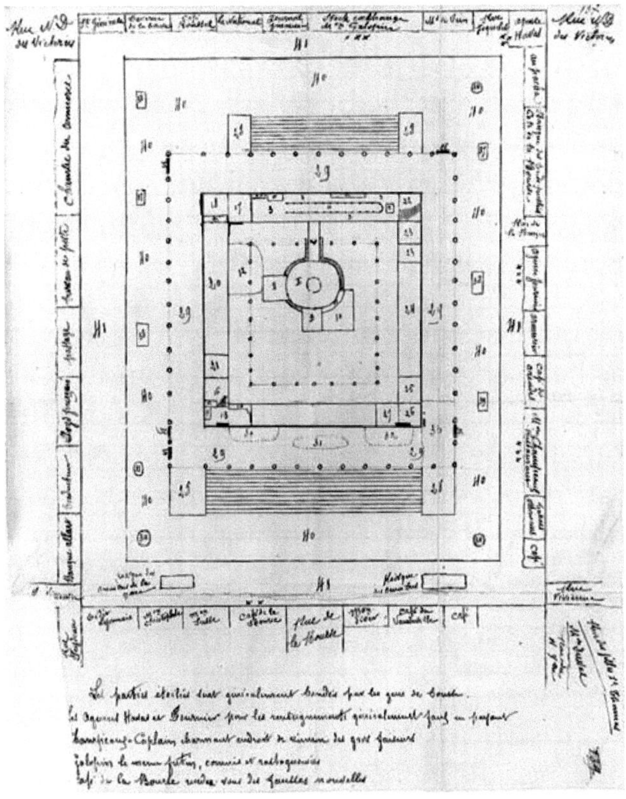

| Plan of the stock exchange drawn up by Zola.

His most meticulous research was carried out when he was preparing to write *The Ladies' Paradise*: he spent over two months in the department stores Grands Magasins du Louvre and Le Bon Marché in order to fully grasp their organisational structure and how they operated. In its detail and thoroughness, Zola's work can almost be described as journalistic. Indeed, in addition to his vast literary output, Zola worked as a journalist, and this no doubt influenced his approach to literature.

This quasi-scientific approach to writing is one of the hallmarks of Zola's work and is inextricably linked to his aims: he wanted his novelistic output to be at least as complete, coherent and meticulous as the real world and the extensively studied events of the 19th century.

MORE THAN A GREAT NOVELIST

As well as his celebrated *Les Rougon-Macquart* series, Zola also wrote tales, poems, plays (notably adaptations of his novels, which met with limited success) and short stories. These included *The Attack on the Mill*, his contribution to the naturalist anthology *Les Soirées de Médan*.

METICULOUS DESCRIPTION AND RIGOROUS CONSTRUCTION

This extensive preparatory work obviously had an impact on Zola's language and writing. After his detailed research, he aimed to depict reality as transparently as possible rather than distorting it with a Romantic, Symbolist or classical style. He saw realist writing as most suitable for this purpose. Consequently, Zola writes his novels as though he were describing a scene from everyday life: he uses long, exceptionally detailed descriptions and adopts an impartial, objective stance to present an unembellished vision of the world. His language is sophisticated and carefully crafted, but always realistic, and it is sometimes adapted to the environments he describes (his characters often talk using slang, like real people).

Zola's work is logically and solidly constructed, on both a microstructural level (his chapters are meticulously arranged) and a macrostructural level (the overall structure of *Les Rougon-Macquart* is based on a clear, defined genealogy, and each novel deals with one or more members of the Rougon-Macquart family). This is the foundation his socio-historical epic is built on: its seamless, beautifully complex, almost symphonic construction allows collective destiny to be emphasised over individual destiny. This characteristic is further accentuated by Zola's extensive and original use of indirect free speech. This style of narration is situated somewhere between direct speech and indirect speech, and is characterised by the absence of an introductory verb of speech ("said", "asked", "thought", and so on). In Zola's work, free indirect speech gives the impression that the novel was written by a vast collective voice.

LITERARY DEVICES AND NETWORKS OF SYMBOLS

Although Zola was a consciously meticulous, methodical writer, he was also a novelist. This means that imagination plays a significant role in his work and that he makes extensive use of literary devices, but always with the aim of serving the truth. While he aims to present an unadorned picture of reality, he chooses particular points of view to make certain details stand out. He also incorporates symbols and symbolic networks into his novels, which create a subtle poetic effect and strengthen the effects of his work. For example, in *Germinal*, the colours red and black, which are linked to iron and coal, are omnipresent.

Furthermore, while working to faithfully depict real life, he also sometimes exaggerates reality until it attains symbolic proportions. His tendency to describe crowds more than individual people is significant in this respect, as it gives his work a powerful epic dimension and emphasises the collective, the crowd and the unity of the people. In this way, Zola shows that, for him, the real heroes are social groups, which, like individuals, can change for better or for worse.

Finally, Zola's work incorporates traditional motifs, stereotypes and archetypes, including the monstrous machine in *The Human Beast*, violence in *Germinal*, sex and fertility in *The Earth* and consumption in *The Ladies' Paradise*. These symbols, which come from the collective imagination and carry echoes of myth, elevate Zola's work to the stature of legend.

MODERN, REVOLUTIONARY THEMES

As a skilled observer of contemporary reality, and influenced by his work as a journalist, Zola focuses on topical themes from the 19th century and grounds each of his novels in the society of the time, describing its overall structure, the day-to-day atmosphere and the living conditions of each of its social classes in minute detail. Specifically, certain themes recur throughout his work:

- **The business world:** from department stores to industry to finance, Zola often depicts the world of the newly wealthy middle classes, whose success frequently conceals the immoral behaviour that allowed them to become rich.
- **Social problems and the world of the working classes:** Zola regularly describes the newly formed working class, which was trying to establish its place in society and assert its rights through strikes and rebellions.
- **The decline of the lower classes:** Paris's less fortunate inhabitants are trampled by the powerful and are gradually driven to madness,

alcoholism, crime and begging. Zola positions himself as a witness to these daily injustices and seeks to describe them objectively.

Zola's novels are often considered to be quite bleak, as they have a very dark atmosphere and rarely end happily for their protagonists. However, although most of his writing tends towards degradation, degeneration and decline, and is largely based on repetition which adds to the darkness of his texts, he ends his work with an image of hope and life. In this way, he proves to his readers that he is still a positivist, meaning that he has faith in progress and wants to contribute to the development of modern society.

Zola believed that novelists should work to bring about reform and that they had a duty to denounce society's flaws and depict truth and fairness in their work in order to pave the way for a better world. In addition to his notable role in the Dreyfus affair, he believed that he had a responsibility towards the people. As a witness to social injustice, and especially as a positivist in favour of progress, he wanted to open his readers' eyes and change their minds in the hope of encouraging them to rebel against inequality

and helping to achieve profound social and economic reform.

NOTABLE WORKS

THÉRÈSE RAQUIN

Thérèse Raquin is Zola's third novel, and was written well before he had the idea for *Les Rougon-Macquart*. It first appeared in serial form, before being published as a book in 1867. Its success marked the beginning of its author's literary career, and it was in this book that Zola laid the foundations for naturalism.

Thérèse has married her weak, sickly cousin Camille, whom she cannot stand, on the insistence of her aunt Madame Raquin. When the three of them move to Paris and she meets the energetic, lively Laurent, she soon gives in to her feelings and becomes his mistress. Shortly afterwards, the two lovers kill Camille, whom they believe to be standing in the way of their happiness, by throwing him into the water while the three of them are out rowing. To begin with, they do not dare to see each other again, but Thérèse manages to persuade Laurent that they will soon forget about the incident and they get married. Unfortunately for them, she was wrong: remorse, resentment, shame, anger and fear eat away at the couple, and one day they openly argue about the murder in front of Madame Raquin, whose health has deteriorated to the point that she is now paralysed. She is horrified when she realises what has happened but, given that she is essentially a prisoner in her own body, she cannot tell anyone or exact revenge on them. The two lovers end up poisoning one another as the powerless old woman looks on.

The novel met with an enthusiastic critical and popular reception. Although Zola was relatively young when he wrote it and was still finding his feet as an author, his text is clearly grounded in the realist tradition. It also features a number of the major characteristics of his mature works: tragic ending, pessimism, the observation of decadence, a meticulous description of social classes, and social and human realism.

Furthermore, even at this early stage in his career, Zola carried out research on the ground before writing his novel. Consequently, his descriptions give the impression of an approach that is more scientific than artistic. The story is meticulously, methodically constructed around the central theme, and the events of the novel follow on logically from the increasing remorse of the two protagonists. The characters' emotions and feelings and their consequences are so closely examined that the novel could almost be a medical study on obsession. The two fundamental components of naturalism, namely psychology and physiology, are already present in this early novel.

THE ATTACK ON THE MILL

The Attack on the Mill was Zola's contribution to *Les Soirées de Médan*, an anthology of six naturalist short stories published in 1880 which brought together some of the most prominent authors of the time: Paul Alexis (1847-1901), Joris-Karl Huysmans (1848-1907), Guy de Maupassant, Léon Hennique (1850-1935) and Henry Céart (1851-1924). The book is often considered to be the manifesto of naturalism and features *Boule de Suif* by Maupassant, an immensely successful short story that contributed to its author's enduring reputation and popularity.

The authors of *Les Soirées de Médan* unanimously

decided that its unifying theme would be the Franco-Prussian War (1870-1871). In line with naturalist principles, each author adopted a detached, objective, realist stance and stripped away the apparent glamour of the war to emphasise the less noble sentiments that accompanied it, such as shame, stupidity, decadence and cowardice. Overall, the collection can be described as anti-war and anti-militarist.

The Attack on the Mill is the first story in the collection and is set at the start of the war, in a small provincial village called Rocreuse. It opens with a party to celebrate the engagement of Françoise, the miller's daughter, to Dominique. Barely a month later, Prussian troops invade the village and seize the mill. The young couple is present for the outbreak of the fighting and looks on as many men are killed and the French are forced to retreat. Dominique, who fought as a marksman, is taken prisoner and sentenced to death, but Françoise talks him into running away. When the Prussians discover that he is missing the next morning, they decide to execute the miller in his place, leaving Françoise facing a terrible dilemma: should she hand over her fiancé to save her father? She is ready to make this sacrifice, but does not have to when Dominique is captured. She had been praying for French reinforcements to arrive, and her prayers are answered just before the execution. However, Dominique and her father are both killed in the ensuing fighting. This bitter victory concludes with the collapse of the mill, which is shot to pieces by the cannons.

Beyond the quasi-personification of the mill (Zola frequently anthropomorphises machines in his writing), the meticulous descriptions of nature and rural life, and the precise portrayal of a particular social setting, it is the story's deeply ambivalent ending that most clearly anchors *The Attack on the Mill* in the naturalist movement. While Zola concludes his novel with the triumph of patriotic and collective values, his main focus is the victory's tragic consequences on the lives of poor rural villagers. Although the French army ultimately triumphs, the portrayal of the destruction caused on a human, familial and social level is painfully realistic. When the mill, which forms the beating heart of Rocreuse, collapses, the entire village is crushed. Françoise's life and the little corner of paradise where she lived are sacrificed on the altar of war.

GERMINAL

Germinal, the 13th novel in the *Les Rougon-Macquart* cycle, is undoubtedly also the best-known and most widely read work in the series. It was written and published in serial form between 1884 and 1885, and appeared as a book in March 1885, although Zola began his research much earlier. It met with immediate popular and critical acclaim, which no doubt contributed to its wide dissemination and lasting reputation.

Étienne, the son of Gervaise Macquart and Auguste Lantier, is a decent, intelligent young man who has just started working in the mines at Monsou, northern France. Conditions in the mines are appalling, and even women and children have to work. He is staying with the Maheu family and soon falls in love with their daughter, Catherine, and begins courting her. Outside of work, he campaigns for workers' rights and even tries to instigate a socialism- and communism-inspired strike. However, the strike is brutally put down and everyone goes back to work. At this point, Souvarine, an amoral anarchist and Étienne's main rival, deliberately causes a flood which traps Étienne and Catherine underground. She dies in the young man's arms, and although he survives, he is profoundly shaken by the experience. He realises that big ideas alone are not enough, and that some form of organisation is necessary. He leaves the mines for Paris, planning to take part in the first social campaigns, and the novel ends with his dreamy vision of a better future.

After the success of *L'Assommoir*, Zola planned to write a novel with the people as its hero and socialism as its guiding principle. He initially considered the Paris Commune, but decided that it was already too far in the past, so he decided to focus on the social activism that was sweeping through French mining towns at the time and on the sacrosanct distinction between the social classes.

He wanted to make his new novel as weighty as possible, so he carried out even more meticulous research than before: he went to live with miners for a month, asked labourers and engineers about their everyday lives and met with strike leaders. He then worked on describing the people's living conditions and their motivations for rebelling precisely and methodically, and also depicted the daily lives of working women, who had left behind their traditional tasks to work outside the home. Beyond pure description, he also made his stance clear through a metaphor comparing the miners' revolts to germination in springtime. Furthermore, "Germinal" is the name of a month in the French revolutionary calendar, corresponding to the time of year when nature is renewing itself and being reborn. In this way, Zola suggests that a better future is possible for the oppressed working class, who should rebel to free themselves from their terrible working conditions and fight for their rights.

Germinal therefore represents Zola's first foray into political and social commitment. He also outlines the moral values (such as dignity for the poor and justice for all) that he believes his contemporaries should adopt to govern the modern world, and highlights a series of fun-damental problems such as poverty, injustice, dignity, suffering and the hardships faced by workers, which had been seen as inevitable and unsolvable until that point. His aim was to try and re-establish a healthy moral order, give the ruling classes food for thought and engender greater mistrust of capitalism, while advocating certain elements of socialism, notably those based on collectivity and equality between classes.

Finally, this vision of a collective struggle gives the novel an epic dimension, and means that contemporary events take on a legendary stature. When *Germinal* was first published, it was enthusiastically welcomed by ordinary people and praised by socialists, and its popularity and influence remain considerable even today.

ZOLA'S LEGACY

Zola's tomb at Montmartre Cemetery, Paris.

Works such as *Germinal*, *The Ladies' Paradise*, *L'Assommoir* and *Nana* are now widely known and recognised as classics of French and world literature. Zola is now viewed as the most emblematic French author of the late 19th century and is studied in virtually all schools in France, as well as on many French degree courses in the UK. In addition to his revolutionary ideas and social commitment, he was a meticulous, talented writer, and his work is a great source of national pride in France.

Zola was fortunate in the sense that his exceptional novelistic talents coincided with a specific historical period characterised by upheaval and the march towards modernity. This gave rise to a spectacular 19th-century epic which crossed time periods, styles and borders to attain mythical proportions. Zola's novels were translated into other languages virtually as soon as they were published, which allowed naturalist ideas to spread across Europe, where they became popular in spite of some detractors.

As well as being immensely popular with ordinary readers, Zola was also admired by critics and by authors and artists around the world. He was seen as the outstanding novelist to look up to throughout the 19th and into the beginning of the 20th century. For example, the English novelist Charles Reade wrote *Drink*, an adaptation of *L'Assommoir*, only a few years after Zola's novel was published. His objective, unpretentious, bleak outlook on society fascinated both readers and critics, as did his commitment to equality and justice, which inspired other writers to take a stance. However, in spite of his resounding popular and critical success, to his great disappointment Zola was never elected to the prestigious Académie Française, and few of his fellow writers emulated his approach. Naturalism quickly fell into decline and died out at the same time as the various participants in the evenings at Médan. In subsequent years, he only won over a few foreign authors, the most notable of whom was the Italian writer Giovanni Verga (1840-1922), one of the leading figures of Verismo, an artistic movement largely inspired by naturalism.

With the emergence and growing popularity of film and television, Zola's works have provided a virtually inexhaustible supply of inspiration for directors, and a total of some 150 film and TV movie adaptations have been made in different countries and in different languages. The first of these, *L'Assommoir* by Ferdinand Zecca, appeared the year of Zola's death. Subsequently, a number of his other works became the subject of more or less faithful adaptations. These include in particular *Nana* (adapted for the cinema by Jean Renoir in 1926 and Christian-Jaque in 1955, and for television by Maurice Cazeneuve in 1981 and Édouard Molinaro in 2001) and *Germinal* (which has been adapted for the cinema many times over the years, from Ferdinand Zecca's film in 1903 to Claude Berri's remarkable 1993 adaptation). Zola's life has also provided ample material for the big screen, for example in William Dieterle's Academy Award-winning 1937 film *The Life of Émile Zola*.

SUMMARY

- Zola was the leading figure of the literary movement of naturalism and one of the most important authors of the late 19th century. He lived during a time of change and upheaval, marked in particular by the rise of capitalism, industrialisation and scientism.

- The march towards modernity inspired the general principles behind his work: by applying the scientific method to novel-writing, he created what he referred to as the experimental novel. He used his novels to observe and experiment on society and individuals affected by particular conditions and events.

- He was a chronicler of society, and provided a meticulous depiction of the world around him and the changes and revolutions it was undergoing. To do this, he carried out extensive research prior to writing each novel, and favoured a realistic, descriptive, objective writing style.

- The vast 20-novel series known as *Les Rougon-Macquart* is Zola's most important work and provides a perfect illustration of naturalist principles. It follows the members of one family over five generations, is based on the concepts of heredity and degeneration, and depicts a range of social classes and environments to form a perfectly coherent whole.

- Zola firmly believed that all writers had a role to play in encouraging social change, denouncing social problems and highlighting truth and justice in their works in order to build a better world.

- Furthermore, the description of crowds and the movement of the masses, which is one of the hallmarks of Zola's writing, gives his work an epic, mythical dimension: what counts for him is unity and collectivity.

- Zola's social commitment can be seen in his life as well as his work. In his later years, he threw his support behind the wrongfully accused Albert Dreyfus during the Dreyfus affair, a major socio-political conflict in France, at significant personal cost.

- Zola met with immense popular and critical success during his lifetime, and nowadays is widely recognised as one of the most important French writers of all time.

We want to hear from you!
Leave a comment on your online library
and share your favourite books on social media!

FURTHER READING

BIBLIOGRAPHY

- Albert, P. (1884-1885) *La Littérature française au XIXe siècle*. Paris: Hachette.

- Ambrière, M. ed. (1990) *Précis de la littérature française du XIXe siècle*. Paris: PUF.

- Batilliat, M. (1931) *Émile Zola*. Paris: Rieder.

- De Beaumarchais, J-P. and Couty, D. (1997) *Grandes Œuvres de la littérature française*. Paris: Larousse.

- Becker, C. (1988) *Émile Zola*: Germinal. Paris: PUF.

- Benoit-Dusausoy, A. and Fontaine, G. (1995) *Dictionnaire des auteurs européens*. Paris: Hachette.

- Bouty, M. (1990) *Dictionnaire des œuvres et des thèmes de la littérature française*. Paris: Hachette.

- Clarac, P. ed. (1961) *Dictionnaire universel des lettres*. Paris: Société d'édition de dictionnaires et encyclopédies.

- Dubois, J. (2000) *Les Romanciers du réel. De Balzac à Simenon*. Paris: Seuil.

- Dumesnil, R. (1995) *Le Réalisme et le Naturalisme*. Paris: Éditions Mondiales/De Gigord.

- (2003) *Encyclopédie de la littérature*. Paris: Librairie Générale française.

- Garrigues, J. and Lacombrade, P. (2004) *La France au XIXe siècle : 1814-1914*. Paris: Armand Colin.

- Grente, G. ed. (1972) *Dictionnaire des lettres françaises. XIXe siècle*. Paris: Fayard.

- Laffont, R. and Bompiani, V. eds. (1994) *Le Nouveau Dictionnaire des auteurs de tous les temps et de tous les pays*. Paris: Laffont.

- De Langenhagen, M-A. and Guislain, G. (2005) *Zola*. Studyrama.

- Lepelletier, E. (1908) *Émile Zola : sa vie, son œuvre*. Paris: Mercure de France.

- Michel, A. et al. (1993) *Littérature française du XIXe siècle*. Paris: PUF.

- Mitterand, H. (2001) *Zola*. Paris: Fayard.

- Mitterand, H. and Vidal, J. (1963) *Album Zola*. Paris: Gallimard.

- Mougin, P. ed. (2012) *Dictionnaire de la littérature française et francophone*. Paris: Larousse.

- Pagès, A. (2014) *Zola et le groupe de Médan : histoire d'un cercle littéraire*. Paris: Perrin.

- Robert, G. (1952) *Émile Zola, principes et caractères généraux de son œuvre*. Paris: Les Belles Lettres.

- Seassau, C. (1989) *Émile Zola, le réalisme symbolique*. Corti.

- Stalloni, Y. (2006) *Dictionnaire du roman*. Paris: Armand Colin.

- Vaillant, A., Bertrand, J-P. and Régnier, P. (2006) *Histoire de la littérature française du XIXe siècle*. Rennes: Presses Universitaires de Rennes.

- Van Tieghem, P. (1968) *Dictionnaire des littératures*. Paris: PUF.

- Zola, E. (1984) *The Attack on the Mill and Other Stories*. Oxford: Oxford University Press.

- Zola, E. (2004) *Germinal*. Trans. Pearson, R. London: Penguin.

- Zola, E. (2014) *Thérèse Raquin*. Trans. Thorpe, A. London: Vintage.

ADDITIONAL SOURCES

- Boursoit, J. and Coullet, P. (2017) *Nana by Émile Zola (Book Analysis)*. Trans. Neal, R. Brussels: Plurilingua Publishing.

- Cerf, N. and Coullet, P. (2017) *Thérèse Raquin by Émile Zola (Book Analysis)*. Trans. Neal, R. Brussels: Plurilingua Publishing.

- Delandmeter, A. (2016) *The Ladies' Paradise by Émile Zola (Book Analysis)*. Trans. Brichard, R. Brussels: Plurilingua Publishing.

- Horne, E. (2016) *Zola and the Victorians: Censorship in the Age of Hypocrisy*. London: MacLehose Press.

- Marotte, E. (2017) *The Belly of Paris by Émile Zola (Book Analysis)*. Trans. Neal, R. Brussels: Plurilingua Publishing.

- Nelson, B. ed. (2007) *The Cambridge Companion to Zola*. Cambridge: Cambridge University Press.

- Perrel, C. (2017) *The Earth by Émile Zola (Book Analysis)*. Trans. Hanna, E. Brussels: Plurilingua Publishing.

- Perrel, C. and Coullet, P. (2017) *The Fortune of the Rougons by Émile Zola (Book Analysis)*. Trans. Hanna, E. Brussels: Plurilingua Publishing.

- Riguet, M. and Biehler, J. (2017) *L'Assommoir by Émile Zola (Book Analysis)*. Trans. Neal, R. Brussels: Plurilingua Publishing.

- Schom, A. (1987) *Émile Zola: A Biography*. London: Queen Anne Press.

- Seret, H. and Lhoste, L. (2017) *Germinal by Émile Zola (Book Analysis)*. Trans. Hanna, E. Brussels: Plurilingua Publishing.

ICONOGRAPHIC SOURCES

- Portrait of Claude Bernard. Royalty-free reproduction picture.

- Portrait of Émile Zola. Royalty-free reproduction picture.

- Plan of the *Les Rougon-Macquart* series produced

by Zola. Royalty-free reproduction picture.

- *J'accuse...!*, letter published in the newspaper *L'Aurore* on 13 January 1898. Royalty-free reproduction picture.

- Plan of the stock exchange drawn up by Zola. Royalty-free reproduction picture.

- Zola's tomb at Montmartre Cemetery, Paris. © Donar Reiskoffer.

www.50minutes.com

Ebook EAN: 9782808005180

Paperback EAN: 9782808005197

Legal Deposit: D/2017/12603/797

Cover image: © *Émile Zola*, Paul Nadar

Digital conception by Primento, the digital partner of publishers.